Weekly Reader Children's Book Club presents

DUCK DUCK

WEEKLY READER
CHILDREN'S BOOK CLUB
This is a registered trademark

DUCK DUCK

Story and Pictures by EDNA MILLER

HOLIDAY HOUSE · NEW YORK

To my sister, Elsie

Duck Duck, the mallard drake, fed each day on the plump grains of wild rice he found growing in the shallow water. He caught minnows and tadpoles by "tipping up" and reaching far down at the deep end of the pond. Food was plentiful and life was easy.

At dusk, when furry creatures came down to the water's edge to drink, Duck Duck flew from the pond to guard his mate as she sat upon her nest.

The nest was made of feathers she had plucked from her downy breast. Leaves and twigs shaped the cradle round and low branches sheltered it. She had laid ten greenish-buff eggs and warmed them with her body for many days until now they were ready to hatch.

Duck Duck landed near the pine that hid his mate and their nest. Calling softly to her, he peered beneath the tree. What had happened to the eggs? Why were leaves and feathers scattered all about? Where was Duck Duck's mate?

On frantic wings he searched the pond and circled the nearby woods. Duck Duck quacked so loudly as he flew above the trees he didn't hear the fox bark twice.

Other creatures heard the sound and knew just what had happened.

When the ground haze rose to the tops of the trees and Duck Duck could no longer see he returned to the nesting site. As he hunted once more through feathers and leaves and broken shells he heard a tiny sound—a timid peep and then another. Four bright eyes peered up at him from beneath the lowest branch. Two of the ducklings had safely hatched and were very much alive.

Duck Duck waddled to the pond. The two ducklings pattered close behind him, and with natal down just barely dry they followed him into the water.

All night long the ducklings stayed close to Duck Duck. They didn't make a sound. They learned how to be still—their first lesson on the pond.

There were more lessons to be learned as the ducklings grew. They followed Duck Duck as he fed on soft parts of plants, seeds and roots that grew along the shore. They found these things good to eat. They learned to catch small crayfish and other wiggling things by reaching beneath the water. Soon they knew who were friends and who were enemies and when they must take flight.

When the first leaves, tipped with color, glided across the pond Duck Duck and the ducklings began to moult and lose their feathers. He and his family now wore a drab brown dress that blended with the autumn reeds and grasses. For weeks they all stayed hidden as there was no escape from danger with most of their flight feathers gone. Then new feathers began to appear from the tops of their heads to the tips of their tails.

One chilly day a flock of ducks flew southward overhead. The ducklings heard them call. Their feathers, now, were grown, shining new and full of flight. Duck Duck watched them go. He would stay and guard the nest—his mate might come again.

As the days grew colder and colder fewer friendly small animals visited the pond though foxes, wildcats and weasels came to drink at the shore.

One day some children came to the pond. "Duck Duck," they called as they threw him bits of bread. Duck Duck even fed from their hands. He was not afraid.

Soon only cattails rimmed the pond. Bright leaves darkened beneath the water and snowflakes fell. The edges of the pond turned to ice. Each day there was less and less open water.

When the last small opening in the
pond had closed Duck Duck could find
no food. The wind piled snow around
him as he huddled near the pine. It also
carried far-off sounds of voices he had
known—the children who had fed him
one day from the shore.

Duck Duck waddled slowly toward the sound of the children's voices. He broke the snow crust many times before he reached the road.

he lifted himself on half-frozen wings.

Looking up

and then far down to see if all was clear

Duck Duck landed in the underbrush
not far from a house and a barn. It was
as if he had known the way before. He
flew to the open barn door.

The barn was still and it was warm. He could see chickens asleep on their nests of straw. There was field corn in baskets and water in a trough. Duck Duck found a comfortable spot and tucking his head under a wing, he fell fast asleep.

Winter passed quickly in the barn. The children came each day with food, sweeping snow or sunshine in as they flung the door wide open. Duck Duck became very tame.

One morning when the sun had warmed the boards beneath his feet and melted snow ran in rivulets outside Duck Duck heard a quacking and flapping of wings overhead. Suddenly he flew from the barn and without looking back he headed for the pond in the woods.

Below him, a female duck, buff brown with blue wing patches rested on the water.

To attract the bird's attention Duck
Duck swam about her. He dipped his
head in the water, tossed a spray over
his back and scooted about in circles.
Half flying, half running across the
open water Duck Duck made little
waves. But the duck he was courting
was a wooden decoy. It bobbed up and
down on the water and never looked
his way.

With paddling feet and beating wings Duck Duck raised himself high in the water. He quacked angrily at the wooden duck who had rejected him. While Duck Duck splashed and thrashed at the painted decoy a mallard hen landed on the pond and moved silently toward him.

Duck Duck barely turned his head to look at her. But as he paddled on serenely he knew that a new mate had come to him.

Leslie A. Lovett

About the Author/Artist

Edna Miller is the creator of the beloved MOUSEKIN books. She became interested in animals at an early age. Growing up in New York City she found the American Museum of Natural History and the Central Park Zoo a substitute for her own menagerie. She studied design and illustration both here and abroad. The mother of a married son, she now lives in Nyack, New York with her husband, Leslie A. Lovett, and his two daughters.